FAIRY TALES

ILLUSTRATED BY
EMELIE LIDEHÄLL ÖBERG

GIBBS SMITH
TO ENRICH AND INSPIRE HUMANKIND

23 22   6 5 4

FAIRY TALES
ILLUSTRATIONS © 2017 EMELIE LIDEHÄLL ÖBERG

SWEDISH EDITION COPYRIGHT © 2016 PAGINA FÖRLAGS AB, SWEDEN.
ALL RIGHTS RESERVED.

ENGLISH EDITION COPYRIGHT © 2017 GIBBS SMITH PUBLISHER, USA.
ALL RIGHTS RESERVED. NO PART OF THIS BOOK MAY BE REPRODUCED BY
ANY MEANS WHATSOEVER WITHOUT WRITTEN PERMISSION FROM THE
PUBLISHER, EXCEPT BRIEF PORTIONS QUOTED FOR PURPOSE OF REVIEW.

GIBBS SMITH
P.O. BOX 667
LAYTON, UTAH 84041

1.800.835.4993 ORDERS
WWW.GIBBS-SMITH.COM

ISBN: 978-1-4236-4662-4

THIS BOOK BELONGS TO

Emelies

LEMONADE

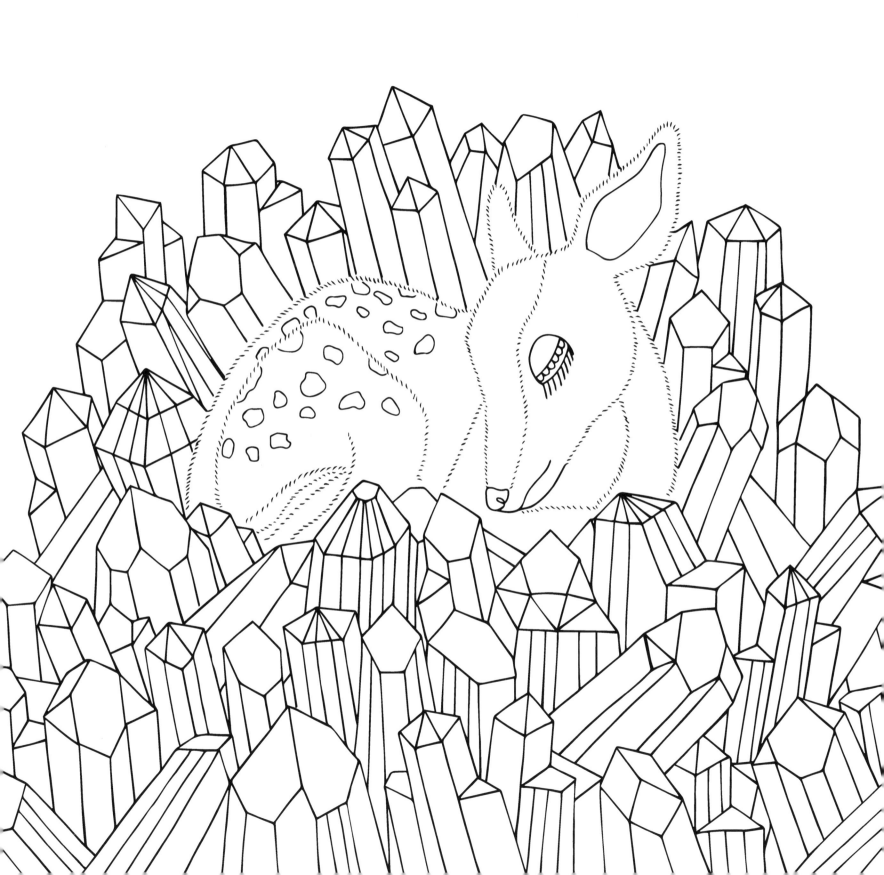

DEER

DEDICATED TO

ELISE